Titanic Survivor

Written by Liz Miles

Illustrated by Amerigo Pinelli

Collins

As I climbed up the steps to the *Titanic*, I felt dizzy.
I never knew a ship could be so enormous!

On deck, we saw an impatient-looking man in uniform. Mum nodded in his direction. "That's the crew's boss!" she said.

Suddenly, the *Titanic*'s horn blew and the passengers cheered. It was so exciting!

Inside, the *Titanic* was a palace! We wandered around and climbed down the grand shiny staircase.

We unpacked our possessions. Then we went to a magnificent room. I made friends with a girl called Florence, and ate a sugary, honeycomb ice cream. It was delicious!

Each night, there were dances and celebrations in the lounge.

Each day, it got colder. I was concerned when I saw icebergs in the sea. "Don't worry!" Mum reassured me.

One night, an unusual noise woke me. I knew the ship was unsinkable, but I still felt very unsure and nervous.

Quickly, I dressed and ran out in the direction of the noise.

"It's all right! Back to your cabin!" shouted a crewman, pushing me away. I knew he was wrong. I saw worry in his face. Had the ship hit something?

Panicking, I ran back to our cabin. Mum was up. I knocked hard on Florence's door. No reply.

Mum grabbed my wrist and wrenched me away.

The musicians still played in the lounge. Yet water whooshed up around the base of the staircase!

My vision was blurred with tears. Where was Florence?
Mum leaned over the rail. "An iceberg!" she screamed.

She shouted crossly at the crewmen, "Has your boss made a decision? Surely, we must get off!"

Life jackets and knapsacks slid across the deck.

At last a lifeboat was ready. Mum jumped in and shouted, "Roger! Hurry!"

I climbed into the boat. It swung dangerously, knocking the side of the ship. Mum coaxed other children, "Get in!"

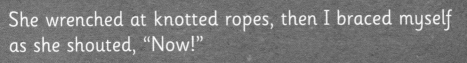

She wrenched at knotted ropes, then I braced myself
as she shouted, "Now!"

The boat fell into the icy water with a bang.

Treasures from the ship bobbed on the surface.

Mum rowed quickly. My knuckles were white with fear. Soon, other boats splashed into the icy water.

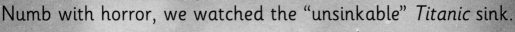

There was a noise like an explosion. Then the gigantic
ship snapped. The front section sank, then the back section.
Numb with horror, we watched the "unsinkable" *Titanic* sink.
I saw no sign of Florence.

Another ship picked us up. We were lucky to be saved.

I sat wrapped in a blanket. Where was Florence?
I knew she might not have escaped.

Then I heard a shout. "Roger!" It was Florence! She had
badly cut her knee on wreckage but she was alive.

I helped look for a little boy's mum. Lots of dads were lost. Men and crew were last off the ship.

At the end of the voyage, we were all numb with shock. Florence had to go to hospital.

Florence soon got better. We knew we would be friends forever. Many people had died on the *Titanic*. We were very lucky.

How is Roger feeling?

After reading

Letters and Sounds: Phases 5–6

Word count: 507

Focus phonemes: /n/ kn, gn /m/ mb /r/ wr /s/ c, ce /zh/ s /sh/ ti, si, ssi, s, ci /c/ x

Common exception words: of, to, the, into, said, were, one, our, people, friends, door, water, many

Curriculum links: History: Events beyond living memory that are significant nationally or globally

National Curriculum learning objectives: Reading/word reading: apply phonic knowledge and skills as the route to decode words, read common exception words, noting unusual correspondences between spelling and sound and where these occur in the word; read other words of more than one syllable that contain taught GPCs; Reading/ comprehension: develop pleasure in reading, motivation to read, vocabulary and understanding by being encouraged to link what they read or hear to their own experiences

Developing fluency

- Your child may enjoy hearing you read the book.
- Take turns to read two to four pages of text, encouraging your child to read spoken words with feeling, and to pause at commas.

Phonic practice

- Focus on words with the following sounds and spellings: kn /n/, gn /n/ mb /m/. Ask your child to sound out the following:

  knotted   knew   numb   sign   honeycomb   knuckles

- Next, focus on words with "wr" spellings. Ask your child to sound out the following:

  wrong   wrenched   wrapped   wreckage

Extending vocabulary

- Look together at words ending in -tion and -sion. Can your child make new words by using one of these two endings?

  celebrate (*celebration*)   explode (*explosion*)   possess (*possession*)   direct (*direction*)

- Discuss how the ending changes the meaning of the root word. (*the verb changes to a noun*)
- How many other -tion or -sion words can your child think of?